MUSEUM MYSTERIES

Museum Mysteries is published by Stone Arch Books
A Capstone Imprint
1710 Roe Crest Drive
North Mankato, MN 56003
www.mycapstone.com

Library of Congress Cataloging-in-Publication Data
Brezenoff, Steven, author. The case of the missing mom / by Steve Brezenoff ;
illustrated by Lisa K. Weber.
        pages cm. -- (Museum mysteries)

Summary: A shipment of dinosaur bones meant for a new exhibit at the Capitol City
Natural History Museum has disappeared, and so have the five paleontologists who were
working late at the museum, including Wilson Kipper's mother - so Wilson and his museum
friends set out to solve the mystery.

ISBN 978-1-4965-2517-8 (library hardcover) -- ISBN 978-1-4965-2521-5 (pbk.)
ISBN 978-1-4965-2525-3 (ebook pdf)

1. Natural history museums--Juvenile fiction. 2. Dinosaurs-Juvenile fiction. 3. Missing
persons--Juvenile fiction. 4. Mothers-Juvenile fiction. 5. Criminal investigation--Juvenile
fiction. 6. Best friends--Juvenile fiction. 7. Detective and mystery stories. [1. Mystery
and detective stories. 2. Natural history museums--Fiction. 3. Musems--Fiction. 4.
Dinosaurs--Fiction. 5. Missing persons--Fiction. 6. Mothers--Fiction. 7. Criminal
investigation--Fiction. 8. Best friends--Fiction. 9. Friendship--Fiction.] I. Weber, Lisa
K., illustrator. II. Title. III. Series: Brezenoff, Steven. Museum mysteries.
PZ7.B7576Cal 2016
813.6--dc23
[Fic]

                                    2015020986

Designer: K. Carlson
Editor: A. Deering
Production Specialist: K. McColley

Photo Credits: Shutterstock (vector images, backgrounds, paper textures)

Printed and bound in China.
10015R

The Case of the
MISSING MOM

By Steve Brezenoff
Illustrated by Lisa K. Weber

STONE ARCH BOOKS
a capstone imprint

Prehistoric Humans

- Little is known about prehistoric humans — mostly because they lived in a time before history was recorded.

- Scientists learn about prehistoric humans by studying the ancient caves they inhabited.

- Evidence suggests that the first humans lived in caves along the southern coast of Africa, a region that provided food as well as warm weather.

- One of the oldest human settlements ever discovered is located at Middle Awash in Ethiopia, where humans lived 160,000 years ago.

- Earth is more than 4.5 billion years old, but modern humans have existed for only a fraction of that time — approximately 200,000 years.

Amal Farah

Raining Sam

Wilson Kipper

Clementine Wim

Capitol City Sleuths

Amal Farah
Age: 11
Favorite Museum: Air and Space Museum
Interests: astronomy, space travel, and building models of spaceships

Raining Sam
Age: 12
Favorite Museum: American History Museum
Interests: Ojibwe history, culture, and traditions, American history – good and bad

Clementine Wim
Age: 13
Favorite Museum: Art Museum
Interests: painting, sculpting with clay, and anything colorful

Wilson Kipper
Age: 10
Favorite Museum: Natural History Museum
Interests: dinosaurs (especially pterosaurs and herbivores) and building dinosaur models

TABLE OF

CONTENTS

CHAPTER 1
New Shipment

It was after closing time at the Capitol City Natural History Museum. Ten-year-old Wilson Kipper sat on the cold tile floor of the dinosaur wing under a high glass ceiling and looked up at the starry sky far above. Beside him stood thirteen-year-old Clementine Wim, one of his closest friends despite their difference in age.

It wasn't just their age difference that made Wilson and Clementine an odd pair. On the surface, the two had almost nothing in common. Wilson never went anywhere without his tablet computer, while Clementine preferred to travel with a pad of thick paper and a tray of watercolors.

Wilson, African-American and barely four feet tall, kept his hair cut as short as possible. It was just easier that way. Clementine Wim, on the other hand, was as pale as the sky on an overcast winter afternoon and already taller than both of Wilson's moms. She almost always wore her long hair — as bright orange as the fruit she was named for — gathered into a sloppy bun on the top of her head.

One thing the two did have in common was the Capitol City Museum Authority.

Wilson's mother, Dr. Kipper, was a paleontologist here at the Natural History Museum, and Clementine's mother worked at the nearby Capitol City Art Museum. That's why they were allowed to hang out here after hours.

Tonight, they were also waiting for Dr. Kipper. She and several of the museum's other scientists were working late, carefully unpacking a shipment from a dig site in China that had arrived that morning. Everyone was very excited about it.

"How does it look so far?" Clementine asked. She took a step or two back from the easel she'd brought from home, along with a canvas and a box of oil paints and brushes. The past several hours, she'd been hard at work on a portrait of the museum's life-size model of the Allosaurus.

Wilson looked up from his tablet. "You mean *she*," Wilson corrected.

"She?" Clementine repeated, confused.

Wilson nodded. "Mom and I call her Allison," he said. "We used to call her Albert, but then we learned the model was based on a female Allosaurus's skeleton, so we changed it to Allison."

"Makes sense," Clementine said, squinting at the model again as if seeing it for the first time. "So how does she look?"

Wilson got to his feet for a better look at the painting. It didn't look like any Allosaurus he'd ever seen — or any other dinosaur for that matter.

"I'm not sure where to start, Clem," Wilson said. "I guess, why is it blue? And pink? And yellow and red and green?"

Clementine smiled but didn't say anything.

"Also, I think that's a triangle with arms, not a dinosaur," Wilson added. It was truly the strangest painting he'd ever seen.

"It's an abstract representation of Allison," Clementine said. She lifted her brush and approached the canvas again, then stopped. "I think it's just about done."

Wilson didn't get it, but then again, he so often didn't. His tablet, sitting on the floor at his feet, let out a bleep, and the little notification light flashed green. "That's probably from Mom," he said as he scooped up the tablet.

"Can you spend the night at C's house?" the message read.

"She wants me to stay at your place tonight," Wilson said.

"No problem," Clementine said as she packed up her paints and brushes. "You know our futon is always open to you."

"Thanks," Wilson said, and he typed back to his mom: *"Clem says OK. How come?"*

A moment later, the reply came: *"I'm going to be here all night. So much to uncover in this shipment! XOXO"*

"OK," Wilson texted back. *"Let me know what's inside when you're all done!"* Then he grabbed his shoulder bag and slipped the tablet inside. "Ready when you are," he said to Clementine.

"What time is it?" Clementine asked as she folded the easel.

"Um," Wilson said, checking his watch, "a little before eight."

"Oops!" Clementine exclaimed. She gathered her things in her arms and hurried from the room. "Come on! My mom's been out front since seven!"

CHAPTER 2
Cause for Concern?

The next morning, Wilson woke to the sound of Clementine humming. He sat up on the futon and saw his friend kneeling on the rug in the middle of the Wims' family room, facing the big window that looked out over the backyard.

"What are you doing?" he said as he stretched.

"Greeting the sun," Clementine said. "Hope I didn't bother you."

Wilson shook his head and yawned. Then he reached off the edge of the futon and checked his phone for a message from his mom. Nothing.

"That's weird," he said.

"What's weird?" Clementine asked.

"I still don't have any messages from my mom," Wilson explained as he dialed. "I better call home."

"I'll make breakfast," Clementine said as she stood up. "I assume mango-wheatgrass smoothies are okay with you?"

"Um . . .," Wilson started to say, but she'd already left the family room.

Just then, someone picked up the phone. "*Allo?*" It was Moman — Creole for *Mom*, which was what Wilson called his other mother. She had a strong French Creole accent. Wilson found it a little embarrassing sometimes, but Clementine thought it was charming.

"Moman, it's me," Wilson said.

"Oh, good morning," she said. "Did you sleep well at your friend's?"

"Pretty good," Wilson said. He had to cover his ear as the blender started whirring in the next room. "I was wondering if Mom came home. I asked her to text me when the shipment was all sorted."

"*Non*," Moman said. "She's been out all night." She laughed a little. "I bet she slept on that little couch in her office. She used to do that all the time in grad school."

"So you're not worried?" Wilson asked.

"Oh, not at all," Moman said. "I'm sure we'll hear something soon — after she's had a strong cup of coffee."

Wilson knew Moman was probably right, but he decided to try Mom's cell phone just in case. The call went straight to voice mail.

Clementine walked in carrying two glasses of pale-green liquid just as Wilson hung up. As soon as she caught sight of his worried face, her smile fell away at once. "No word from your mom?" she asked.

Wilson shook his head. "And her phone is off, I guess," he said. "I tried to call her, but it went straight to voice mail."

"Maybe her battery died in the night," Clementine said as she set the glasses on the coffee table. "Happens to my mom all the time."

Wilson lay back on the futon and stared at the ceiling. *But my mom isn't like that,* he thought. And deep down, he couldn't shake the feeling that something terrible had happened.

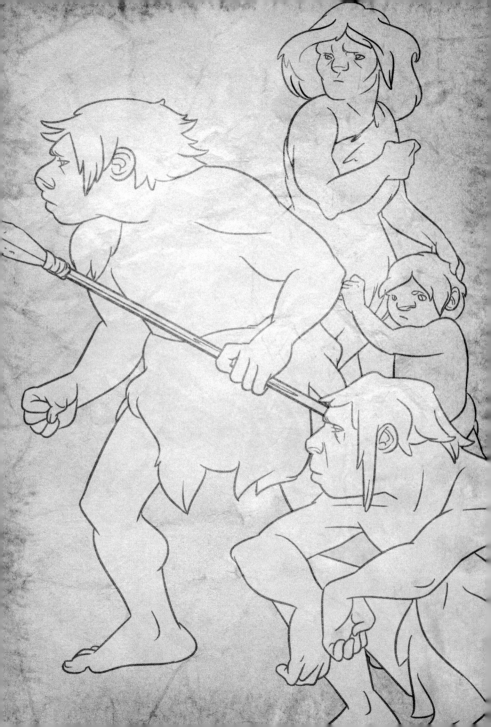

CHAPTER 3
Missing Mom

It was a cool and sunny Saturday morning, so Wilson and Clementine decided to walk to the Natural History Museum. The whole way there, Wilson tried his mother's cell phone again, but every call went straight to voice mail.

"It's almost nine o'clock," Wilson said. After one last try, he shoved his phone into his pocket. "The museum is going to open in a few minutes. She *must* be awake by now."

"But does she have a phone charger at work?" Clementine asked.

"At work, in her car, in Moman's car, in her home office, in the kitchen . . . " Wilson's voice trailed off. "She is never without a charger."

"Wow," Clementine said as the four Capitol City museums came into view at the top of the hill. "That is a lot of chargers. She could lead a cavalry."

Wilson knew Clementine was making one of her weird jokes that he didn't get, but he didn't care. He was too worried for jokes. "She didn't answer her office phone either," he said. "I just hope she's in the lab. Maybe she's still asleep on the couch in there."

As they approached the Natural History Museum, Wilson spotted Raining Sam and Amal Farah, his other two best friends and the children of two more museum employees. He'd texted them both before leaving Clementine's and asked them to meet up.

"Are they open yet?" Wilson called ahead to his friends.

Raining shook his head, and a moment later Theo, one of the museum security guards, appeared on the other side of the revolving front door. He knelt down and unlocked it.

"Come on," Wilson said. He led his friends through the revolving door, not even stopping to greet Theo. He ran right past the ticket booth.

"Sorry!" Clementine hollered over her shoulder as she, Raining, and Amal hurried after him. "He's really worried about Dr. Kipper."

"Don't worry!" Kathy, the ticket seller that morning, called after them. "You're all good to go. I'll print your free tickets and collect them for you too."

"Thanks!" Wilson's three friends said as they ran on.

Wilson hardly registered any of the exchange. He was too focused on finding his mom. He hurried toward the central courtyard, past the animatronic dinosaurs, and through the doors on the far side labeled MUSEUM EMPLOYEES ONLY.

Heading down the hallway, Wilson poked his head into his mom's office. She wasn't there. He knew she wouldn't be, but he had to check. Next stop — the lab. That's where Dr. Kipper and the other museum scientists had been opening that shipment from China last night.

Wilson glanced over his shoulder to make sure Clementine and the others were still behind him. They were — he wasn't the fastest of the group, after all. He headed deeper into the employees-only section of the museum, past other offices and archive rooms. Far at the back of the last hallway, just before the service elevator, the doors to the paleontology lab stood wide open. The lights were on.

Wilson ran into the room. "Mom?" he called, though he saw no one. Even the crates from China were gone. "Mom, are you here?"

Six feet hurried in behind him. Wilson felt Clementine's arm around his shoulders, but he wiggled away and ran toward the back of the lab, where the scientists took their coffee breaks.

"Mom?" he called again, but the two couches were empty, and the coffee cups on the little table were cold. Wilson looked around the space, confused and concerned. "She's not here."

Clementine appeared next to him. "I'll call Moman," she said, reaching for the phone next to the coffee table.

But Wilson shook his head. "No," he said, taking out his own phone. "I'll call the police."

CHAPTER 4
Stolen Property

"I don't understand," Wilson said from his seat on the couch at the back of the lab. He'd been on the phone with the police department for the past twenty minutes. "People are missing. That makes them missing people, doesn't it?"

"Not to us," the police detective said. "An adult isn't officially considered missing until she's been gone for forty-eight hours."

"But she's been gone for fourteen hours," Wilson said. "I mean, that's the last time I heard from her."

"Sorry," the detective said. "There's nothing I can do."

Raining, who sat on the edge of the coffee table in front of Wilson, suddenly started bouncing with excitement. "Ooh!" he said. "Ooh! The China shipment!"

"What?" Wilson said.

"The shipment!" Raining said, bouncing to his feet. "It's gone too!"

"What was that?" the detective asked. "Was something stolen?"

"Oh, yes," Wilson said. "My mother and the other doctors were unpacking a shipment from a dig in China. It seems to be gone too."

"Huh," the detective said. "That we can investigate. Stolen property doesn't have any time constraints. I assume you weren't the owner of the shipment?"

"No," Wilson said. "The museum owns it, I guess."

"I'll have to speak to a museum representative, then," the detective said.

Wilson stood up. "Okay," he said. "I'll get someone for you. Will you hold on?" He took off like a shot, sprinting through the back halls of the museum toward the president's office. He reached her just as she was arriving for the day.

"Mrs. Nakamoto," Wilson said breathlessly. "Phone for you. It's the police." He handed over his cell phone.

"Um, hello, Wil—" she started to say. "What are you—? Hello? Police? Missing? Stolen? Oh my goodness . . . yes, send someone over right away!"

Wilson leaned on the wall and gasped for breath as his friends joined him. Clementine took his hand and squeezed it.

"It'll be okay, Wilson," she said. "They'll find your mom. I promise."

Wilson wanted to believe Clementine, but the truth was, he had never been so sad — or unsure — in his life.

CHAPTER 5
Time to Worry

After they hung up with the police, Wilson called Moman back. She was very worried to hear the police were involved and told him to stay put — she was on her way to the museum and would be there soon.

Now there was nothing to do but wait. Wilson sat with Clementine in the museum president's office — her couch

was much nicer than the ones in Dr.
Kipper's office and the paleontology lab.
Raining and Amal decided to stroll through
the museum together.

"We have to help," Amal said. She
turned to Raining and fixed her eyes on
him. "You know that, right?"

"Of course we do," Raining said, but he
couldn't look back at her. He was too upset,
too angry, and too worried about Wilson
and Dr. Kipper. "This is our most important
mystery ever."

"So what do we do first?" Amal asked
as they came to a stop in the middle of the
Prehistoric Humans exhibit. Nearby, statues
of men squatted by an electric campfire in
an imitation cave. The wall behind them
featured a colorful sunset painted with
shades of pink, orange, yellow, and blue.

Raining had passed by the exhibit dozens of times, but he'd never really paid it much attention. Usually he and his friends wandered the dinosaur sections of the museum, or the ancient insects, or even the giant mammals. This part was pretty boring.

"Let's think. What do we know so far?" Raining asked.

"We know Dr. Kipper is missing," Amal said. "And so are the other paleontologists who were working on that China shipment. There were four of them, besides her, I think."

"And the shipment is missing too," Raining pointed out.

"So who would take five people," Amal said, "and a bunch of crates of dinosaur bones and stuff?" She thought about it for a moment. "Maybe another museum? Maybe they needed some brilliant scientists and some decent exhibits, so they decided to take them!"

"If Wilson were here, he could add that to the idea list in his tablet," Raining said.

Amal nodded and frowned. Then she pulled a folded-up piece of paper from her back pocket and a pencil nub from her front pocket. "We'll have to make do with this," she said, scribbling *Another Museum?* at the top of the paper.

"Any other ideas?" Raining said. "I think it was terrorists. Russians or something."

"Terrorists?" Amal said. "Why would terrorists do this? You've been watching too many movies."

"Because terror — duh," Raining said. "They make terror. Isn't this terror?"

"I guess," Amal admitted. "But I don't think it was Russians. I think China is our biggest competition now."

Raining shook his head. "It wouldn't be China," Raining said. "The shipment came from China."

"Oh, yeah," Amal said but then added, "I still say Chinese terrorists. Or another museum. Maybe a museum in China!"

Raining sighed. "Maybe we should head back," he said. "We could use some fresh ideas."

Amal shrugged. "You're probably right," she said. "Not to mention Wilson's brain."

"I just hope it's working," Raining said.

"You hope what's working?" Amal asked.

Raining took Amal's hand and pulled her away from the exhibit. "Wilson's brain."

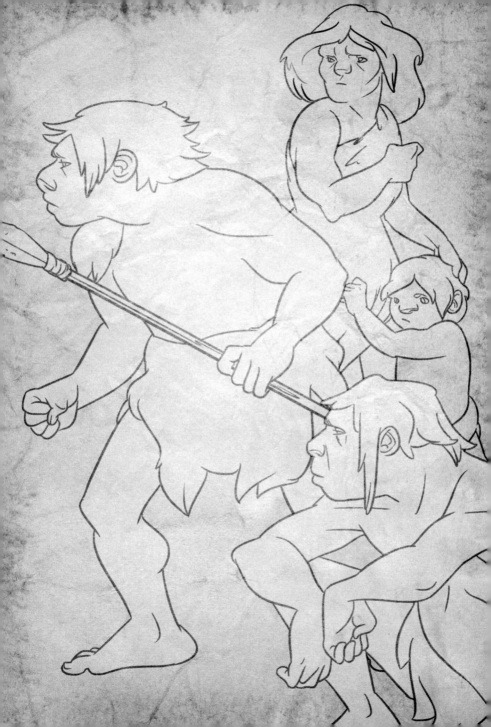

CHAPTER 6
Hunting for Clues

Back in the president's office, Clementine kept one arm wrapped around Wilson's shoulders. After talking to Moman, he'd grown even more upset.

"What are we going to do?" Wilson asked.

"I guess we wait for Moman and the police," Clementine said. "They'll find your mom, Wilson."

Just then, a soft *tap tap* came from the door, and Raining poked his head in. "Can we come in?"

"Of course," Wilson said, but he didn't look up. He just stared at his hands in his lap. They could tell he'd been crying.

Amal and Raining sat in the two chairs facing the president's couch.

"You okay?" Raining asked.

Wilson just shrugged.

"We're going to solve this for you," Amal said, trying to be chipper. "Raining and I already have some ideas."

"What ideas?" Wilson said, finally looking up from his hands.

"Terrorists," Raining said. "Probably Russian."

"Guys," Clementine whispered, shooting them a pointed look.

"Or Chinese," Amal added.

"You guys, come on," Clementine whispered a little louder.

"Or maybe it was a different museum who wanted your mom to work for them," Amal offered. "And they wanted the stuff in the crates for their museum too."

"A Chinese museum," Raining added.

"Okay, that's enough," Clementine snapped. "This isn't helping, and Wilson is very upset. The police will find Dr. Kipper before we know it."

"No," Wilson said. "It's okay. I think they're right."

"You do?" Amal and Raining said.

"Not about the terrorists — or the Chinese museum," Wilson clarified. "But they're right that we need to try to solve this."

"Don't you think we should wait for the police?" Clementine suggested.

"I can't just sit here," Wilson said. "If we're trying to solve the mystery, at least I'll feel like I'm . . . *doing* something."

Clementine gave his shoulders an extra squeeze. "Okay," she said. "Let's go, then." She stood up. Amal and Raining followed her lead and got to their feet as well.

"Yeah, let's go," Amal said. "Let's go find your mom!"

* * *

"Are the police here yet?" Wilson asked as they left the president's office together.

"I don't think so," Raining said. "At least we didn't see them yet."

"Good," Wilson said. "Our first stop is the paleontology lab, then."

"Weren't we there already?" Amal said.

"Yes," Wilson said, "but we didn't look for clues. We might have missed something important."

The four friends hurried down the back hallways to the lab. On the way, they passed Mrs. Nakamoto.

"Oh!" she said. "Wilson, are you sure you don't want to stay in my office till Babet gets here?"

"No, I'm okay," Wilson said. "My friends are, um, helping me keep my mind off everything for now."

The president smiled at him. "Okay, then, dear. You let me know if you need anything at all, though."

"I will," Wilson agreed with a grateful nod.

Mrs. Nakamoto started to head off, but Raining called after her: "Mrs. Nakamoto? Did you just get a new caveman exhibit?"

The museum president shook her head. "I don't think so," she said. "Why?"

"The two cavemen at a campfire in a cave," Raining said. "Something seemed different to me."

"Oh, we've had that for years," Mrs. Nakamoto said, chuckling a bit. "Mr.

Snelling in maintenance probably wishes we didn't have it. The bulb in that fire burns out twice a week!"

"Oh, okay," Raining said, frowning. "I thought for sure something looked new about it. Thanks, anyway."

With that, the president said goodbye and headed back to her office. The kids headed the other direction, where a mystery was waiting to be solved.

CHAPTER 7
A Guilty Friend?

"Darn," Wilson said when they arrived at the lab. The whole thing was now blocked off by yellow police tape. "Now we won't be able to check over the lab for evidence."

"I'm sure the police will find the evidence," Clementine pointed out.

"But then *I'm* not helping," Wilson said. "I want to help."

Just then, a female detective inside the lab spotted the kids in the doorway and headed over to them. "Everything all right out here?" she asked.

"Oh, yes, sorry," Clementine said as she tried to shuffle her friends away from the crime scene. "We'll stay out of your way, detective."

"Just a moment," the woman said. "Is one of you Wilson Kipper?"

Wilson nodded and raised his hand. "I am."

"Your mother is Dr. Carolyn Kipper?" the detective asked.

Wilson nodded, and the detective lifted the crime scene tape. "I'm Detective Gina Pagalucci. Come in here a moment."

Wilson glanced at Clementine and then stepped under the yellow tape and into the lab.

"You'll be able to identify items, if we found something belonging to your mother, right?" the detective asked.

"I guess so," Wilson said. He let the detective lead him away from his friends toward the back of the lab. She stopped beside the coffee table.

"Take a look under the table, but don't touch anything," the detective said. "I don't want to disturb the crime scene. At least until our department photographers get here."

"But I've already been in here," Wilson said as he dropped to all fours to look under the coffee table. "I sat on the couch and called the police."

"We must do the best we can to leave things as they are, even so," the detective said. "Do you see it?"

Wilson nodded. "It's my mom's phone," he said. "Should I grab it?"

"No, leave it just where it is," she said. "You're sure it's your mom's?"

Wilson stood up. "Yes, it's hers," he said. "Is that all?"

"Have you spent much time in the lab?" the detective asked.

"Some," Wilson said. "Not as much as the doctors, obviously."

"Obviously," the detective said. "But I want you to look around — don't touch anything — and tell me if anything looks off. Do you know what I mean?"

Wilson nodded and began to move slowly through the huge room. He walked between bookcases and sample cabinets, past partially constructed models, and alongside the long table of microscopes and light boxes, until he reached the big table near the front of the lab. The edge of that table and a big stretch of floor were covered in a great splat of blue paint.

"This is weird," Wilson said, kneeling beside the table. He glanced at his friends too. They were close-by, right in the doorway still.

"The paint?" the detective said. "I wondered about that. Not much call for that much blue paint in the paleontology lab, is there?"

"No," Wilson said. "Especially right here."

"Why right here?" the detective asked.

"Because this is where they unpack fossils," Wilson explained, standing up. "Most of them are very fragile. The doctors take special care of everything they unpack. They'd never just leave a bunch of paint around."

"Hmm," the detective said. "You're right. That's odd. Have you seen anyone around the museum with blue paint lately?"

"*Ahem,*" said Clementine from the doorway. She raised her hand slowly.

"Yes?" the detective said as she stepped toward Clementine. "Have you seen someone with paint?"

"Well, not *seen* exactly," Clementine said slowly.

"Miss," the detective said, putting her fists on her hips. She looked very powerful and a little scary. "Explain yourself at once."

"I had paint," Clementine admitted. "Last night, here in the museum."

The detective squinted at her. "You did?"

Clementine nodded.

"Why?" the detective asked.

"Because I was painting," Clementine said as if it was self-explanatory.

The detective sighed. "Painting what?"

"A picture," Clementine said. "Of a dinosaur."

"It didn't look like a dinosaur, though," Wilson put in. "It looked like—"

"Okay, that's enough," the detective interrupted. "What's your name, miss?"

"Clementine," she said.

"Last name?"

"Wim."

"Fine," the detective said as she scribbled Clementine's name in her notebook. "I'll want to speak to you more later." She slipped her pad into the pocket of her suit jacket. "You kids run along now. The forensic team will be here soon."

The detective held the tape up, and Wilson ducked back underneath. "Thanks for your assistance," she said. "I'm sure we'll have your mom back, safe and sound, very soon."

"Thanks," Wilson said. He led his friends away from the lab and into the main part of the museum.

Clementine put an arm around his shoulders, but to Wilson's surprise, this time *she* was crying. "Clem, what's the matter?" he asked.

Clementine answered, but her words were muffled by sobs and hiccups as she stopped and held her teary face in her hands.

"Clementine," Amal said, placing a hand on the girl's back. "Why are you so upset?"

"Are you worried about my mom?" Wilson asked.

"Of course I am," Clementine said. She wiped her eyes with the back of her hand. "But that's not why I'm crying . . ." Her words melted into a great, horrible sob.

"Why are you crying, then?" Raining said.

Clementine coughed and sniffed and took a deep breath. "The detective," she said with a wail, *"thinks I did it!"*

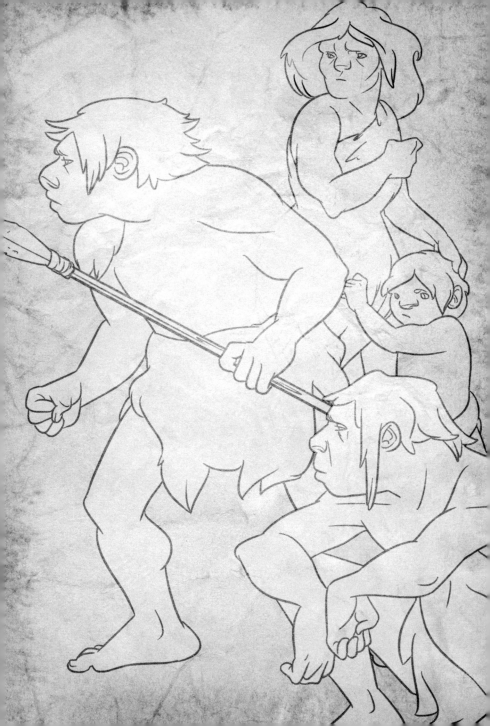

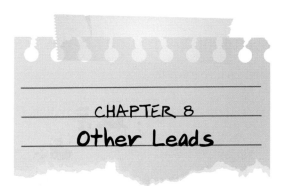

CHAPTER 8
Other Leads

A few minutes later, the four friends found a seat on the wooden bench in the middle of the Prehistoric Humans exhibit. It was quiet there, and it gave Clementine a chance to calm down.

"I really don't think she considers you a suspect, Clem," Wilson said.

"Of course she doesn't think that," Amal agreed. "How could it be you? Five scientists and like ten giant crates? All on your own? It's crazy."

Clementine sniffed. "You think so?"

"No way," Wilson said. "She doesn't think you did it. She just wants to know where the paint came from. She doesn't think you kidnapped my mom."

"Okay," Clementine said. She sniffed again and blew her nose. "Sorry for blubbering."

Wilson gave her shoulders a squeeze. "Let's find Moman," he said. "She must be in Mrs. Nakamoto's office by now."

Sure enough, when the friends arrived back at Mrs. Nakamoto's office, Moman was there waiting. She sat on the couch with her knees together and facing the door. Her eyes were red from crying, and when she saw Wilson, she opened her arms for him. *"Mon cheri,"* she said. *"Mon petit cheri."* Then she started crying again.

"Hi, Moman," Wilson said, walking over to the couch and letting her hug him.

"My darling," Moman said. "I'm sorry it took me so long to get here, and I'm sorry I didn't believe you this morning that something was wrong, and I'm sorry I—"

"Moman," Wilson said, interrupting her. "It's okay. They'll find her. I'm sure they will."

Moman nodded and hugged him a little closer. "I'm here now," she said. "Are you okay?"

Wilson nodded and pulled out of her hug. "I'm going to take a walk," he said. "With my friends."

Moman looked up as if seeing Clementine, Raining, and Amal for the first time. "Thank you for taking such good care of *mon cheri*," she said to them.

"You're welcome," the friends all said together.

"Don't be gone too long, okay?" Moman said.

"Okay," Wilson agreed. He moved back toward the door and pulled Clementine by the hand out of the president's office. Amal and Raining hurried after him.

"Where are we going?" Clementine asked.

"We have to get out of here," Wilson said, hurrying down the hall.

"Why?" Raining said.

"I just don't want to be here," Wilson said. "Where should we go?"

Amal twisted her mouth. "We won't be able to solve the case if we're not even here," she pointed out.

Wilson took a deep breath. "We can look into other leads," he said.

"Like terrorists?" Raining said.

"Chinese museums?" Clementine suggested.

"Shipping companies," Wilson said firmly. "Come on."

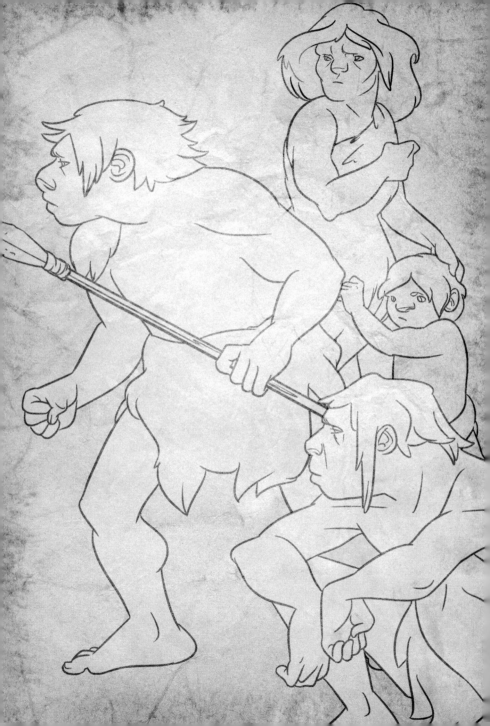

CHAPTER 9
Fly-by-Night

After some poking around at the loading docks behind the museum, Wilson managed to convince one of the shipping assistants to give them the name of the company that delivered the crates from the airport to the museum.

"Fly-by-Night Shipping?" Amal said, reading the slip of paper the shipping assistant had given Wilson. "That's really the name?"

Wilson shrugged. "I guess it's supposed to be funny," he said. "But it checks out. I found their website. Doesn't seem like a huge operation."

"Probably cheap," Raining said. "All the museums are short on funds."

The four kids nodded together. They'd all heard from their parents about what a tough financial situation the Capitol City Museum Authority was in.

"So are you going to call them?" Raining asked, giving Wilson a gentle elbow in the ribs.

"Me?" Wilson said. "I have the youngest voice out of all of us. Clementine should call. She sounds the oldest."

"Me?" Clementine said. "Fine. Give me your phone." Her own phone was often missing or lost or out of batteries or covered in paint. Once she'd baked it right into a ceramic pot.

Wilson dialed and handed the phone and the slip of paper to Clementine. After a moment, she said, "Oh, hi. Is this the shipping company? Do you know what happened to all those bones from China?"

Amal shot Clementine an are-you-serious look and grabbed the phone from out of her friend's hand. With a dramatic roll of her eyes, Amal took over.

"Forgive my assistant," she said, imitating her father's Somali accent in a very distinguished-sounding way. "She's never used a phone before. I'm calling from the Natural History Museum."

Clementine glanced at the boys and shrugged.

"As you may have heard," Amal continued, "a major shipment has gone missing. Of course we're all cooperating with a major police investigation . . . oh? You've already spoken to the police? I see. Well, can you tell me what you told the police? Of course. Thank you."

Amal hung up, looking disappointed. "Well, that didn't work," she said, handing the phone back to Wilson. "They said they'd already talked to the police, and if I'm really calling from the museum then I could ask the police any questions I have."

Wilson sighed. "Great, then we're at a dead end," he said. "No leads. No suspects. And no Mom."

CHAPTER 10
Stumped

Ten minutes later, Wilson, Clementine, Raining, and Amal all sat together, dejected and out of ideas, on the bench in front of the caveman models. They were all completely stumped.

"Jeez," Clementine said, studying the wall in front of them, "I'm not one to speak negatively about any artist's work, but that mural is terrible."

Wilson looked up at the mural of a sunset — the same one Raining had noticed earlier. "I've never seen it before," he said. "It must be new."

"New and terrible," Clementine said. "The lines are sloppy. The paint is uneven" — she walked over to the mural and pointed at several spots — "and the colors are atrocious. They make me feel a little sick — not the feeling a sunset should give you."

Just then, a man in a green jumpsuit walked into the Prehistoric Humans chamber. He had a chain of keys on his belt, along with a series of tools. "How are you holding up, Wilson?" the man asked, stopping in front of the bench.

"Hi, Matthew," Wilson said. "I'm okay, I guess."

"We'll get her back," Matthew said. "You'll see."

"I know," Wilson said, nodding and trying to sound positive. "Hey, do you know when this painting was done?"

Matthew turned and looked at the mural as if he was seeing it for the first time. "Huh," he said. "Well, that wouldn't be my department. You should speak to Hannah in the exhibit maintenance department."

"Aren't you in maintenance?" Wilson asked.

"I'm in *building* maintenance," Matthew clarified. "Not exhibit maintenance. See you later, kids." With that, he walked on toward the cafeteria.

"That reminds me," Raining said. "It's lunchtime."

"I can't eat," Wilson said. "You go ahead."

"Come on," Clementine pleaded. "I'll buy you an ice cream."

Wilson sighed, but he stood up and joined his friends. They decided to have ice cream for lunch. They figured their parents would understand — everyone was having a hard day.

Clementine strode up to the cashier with the four treats while the others grabbed their favorite table — the one near the window, looking out over the courtyard.

"How's Wilson?" the cashier asked Clementine as she paid.

Clementine looked over at her friend. "He's pretty upset," she said. "I just wish I could help."

"I'm sure you're helping," the woman said, "just by being around. That's six dollars and forty cents."

Clementine gave her a ten-dollar bill — accidentally handing the cashier the slip of paper with the words *Fly-by-Night Shipping* written on it. "Oh, oops," Clementine said. "That's not money."

The cashier read it out loud. "I know that name," she said as she handed the paper back to Clementine. "Oh, yes! I saw that truck today at the Highway and Byway — the motel on Route Ten."

"You did?" Clementine said.

"Yup," the cashier said as she handed over Clementine's change. "I dropped off my son. He works there.

There was a truck parked in the back lot with *Fly-by-Night Shipping* printed on the side."

"Thank you!" Clementine said, shoving her change into her pocket. "Thank you very much!" She hurried toward her friends.

"Don't forget your ice cream!" the cashier called after.

"Thanks," Clementine said, and she tossed the four treats into a white paper bag. "I think I'll have them to go."

* * *

"How will we get there?" Wilson said, almost breathless, as he hurried to keep up with his friends as they dashed through the museum toward the front exit.

"Bikes," Clementine said. "We'll bike."

"Yours is at your house," Wilson said. "And mine is at my house."

"And we got a ride from my dad," Raining said.

"We'll call a cab, then," Clementine said. "Come on!"

At the exit, though, they all stopped short. Standing at the main doors — accompanied by a gang of officers in blue uniforms — was Detective Pagalucci.

"Well, well, well," the detective said when she saw the four friends approaching. She crossed her arms and blocked the doors. "If it isn't our resident painter, Clementine Wim. Where do you think *you're* going?"

CHAPTER 11
Stakeout

"Um . . .," Clementine started to say, but all other words escaped her. She slipped back between her friends, as if she could hide behind them. It was impossible, of course, even if she weren't the tallest one by six inches.

"Our forensic team ran tests on the paint we found splattered in the paleontology lab," the detective said as she stepped closer to Clementine. She pulled out her notebook and read: "Artificial pigment suspended in an acrylic polymer emulsion marketed at department stores as Posh Midnight Blue."

Clementine held her breath and thought frantically. *Artificial pigment. Acrylic polymer emulsion . . .*

"Oh!" she exclaimed gleefully. "Oh! Acrylic! It's acrylic paint! I never use acrylics! I use oils and watercolors and egg tempera, but I *never* use acrylics!"

"Of course you don't," the detective said, smiling. "It's a house paint. I'm sure you have nothing to do with the big paint spill in the lab. This paint is from one of the cans missing from building maintenance."

"Really?" Clementine said. "Oh, I'm so relieved. Thank you!"

"Now then," the detective said. "Where are you four going?"

Clementine looked at Wilson. Wilson looked at Raining. Raining looked at Amal. Amal groaned.

"Detective Pagalucci," Amal said, "can you give us a ride?"

* * *

Twenty minutes later, Raining, Wilson, and Amal sat in the backseat of the detective's unmarked police car. Clementine, with the longest legs, sat in the passenger seat up front.

"This car sure has a lot of gadgets," Clementine remarked. She was tempted to poke the computer screen that hovered between the two front seats but kept her hands to herself. With her luck it probably would have set off a siren or fired a missile from the headlights or dropped an oil slick from the rear license plate.

"I still don't understand how you four tracked down the missing truck," the detective said as she turned into the motel's parking lot.

"Just got lucky," Clementine said with a shrug.

"All right," the detective said. "I'm going to speak to the motel manager. You and your friends stay in the car. Got it?"

Clementine nodded. "Got it."

The detective set her with an icy, long stare. "I mean it. Stay here."

"Will do!"

"Good," Detective Pagalucci said. "I'll be back." With that, she climbed out and closed the door.

The four friends watched as Detective Pagalucci walked up to the main building and stepped into the motel's office. As soon as the door swung shut behind the detective, Amal opened the back door of the car. "Let's go check the truck," she said.

"But I just told the detective we'd stay here!" Clementine protested.

"No," Amal pointed out. "You said *you'd* stay here. You didn't say anything about the rest of us."

"Ugh," Clementine said with a groan. "Fine — but hurry!"

"Will do!" said Amal as she, Raining, and Wilson climbed out of the car.

Clementine watched them run toward the back of the motel and the rear parking lot. "They better be careful," she muttered to herself. She fixed her eyes on the office door and kept her fingers crossed that Detective Pagalucci would be in there for a long, long, *long* time.

CHAPTER 12
Motel Mistake?

"It's probably locked," Wilson said as he, Amal, and Raining approached the truck parked in the lot behind the motel. Sure enough, the words on the side of the vehicle said *Fly-by-Night Shipping*.

Amal heaved the opening mechanism, and the door rolled up with a tremendous boom. "Not locked," she said triumphantly.

Wilson ran over to look inside. "Empty, though," he said.

"Let's get back to the car," Raining said. "The detective will be back soon."

Before they could make a move, though, a booming voice shouted: "Hey! What are you doing?"

There was nowhere to run, so the three kids just stood there and watched as a man stomped through the open doorway of a nearby motel room. "Get away from that truck!"

"Sorry!" Wilson said. "We didn't mean anything by it!"

"Oh, no?" the man said. He stomped right up to them. He was big and mean looking, and he hadn't shaved in days. He smelled of body odor and Chinese food. "You always open up the backs of trucks that don't belong to you?"

"All trucks don't belong to us," Raining said. "We don't have any trucks."

"What?" the man said.

"Never mind."

"Excuse me!" someone shouted. It was Detective Pagalucci. She and the motel manager were hurrying across the parking lot toward them. "I thought I told you kids to wait in the car."

"We thought you just meant Clementine," Amal said quickly.

"Why would I just mean Clementine?" the detective said. "Get back in the car!"

Raining and Wilson headed for the car, but Amal grabbed their wrists. The detective wasn't watching them anymore, and Amal wanted to see what was about to go down.

Detective Pagalucci stepped up to the mean-looking man. "Are you the driver from Fly-by-Night Shipping?" she asked.

The mean-looking man suddenly looked way less mean. "Yes," he said. "I mean, I'm one of them. My partner is napping."

"That's your room?" Detective Pagalucci said, pointing at the open door in the motel.

"Yeah."

"Let's go have a look," the detective said. She walked right for the door, not even waiting for its occupant. The manager hurried after her, and so did Amal, Wilson, and Raining.

"Just a minute!" called the man from the shipping company. "My partner is napping in there!"

"Then we'll wake him up," said the detective. True to her word, she thumped her fist on the open motel room door, pushed it open, and strode into the room. "Wakey, wakey!"

Amal poked her head into the room just as the other driver sat up in one of the two twin beds.

"Guh?" said the wakened man. "What's going on?"

"Just going to have a look around," Detective Pagalucci answered. She moved quickly through the room, looking in the closet and the bathroom. It was a very small room, so it didn't take long. "Nothing suspicious here."

"Of course there isn't!" said the driver who'd come in from

outside. "Why would there be anything suspicious?"

"Surely you've heard that the shipment you left at the museum yesterday has been stolen," the detective said.

"It has?" the driver said. "That's terrible!"

"It sure is," the other driver agreed as he lay back down. "It was really heavy too. When they find it, we're not moving it again." In a moment, he was snoring.

"Sorry," said the first driver. "We were up pretty late last night."

"A late-night delivery?" Raining asked.

"No," the driver said, laughing. "Just these thin motel walls, you know." He looked at the detective. "Is there anything else?"

"I guess not," Detective Pagalucci said. "But don't leave town just yet, all right?"

"You got it," said the driver. "Maybe I'll grab a nap too." With that, he closed the door, leaving the kids, the detective, and the motel manager on the sidewalk.

"Didn't you say this room was a single?" the detective asked, turning to the hotel manager.

The manager stammered and scratched his chin. "Must be a mistake with the computer," he said. "The night manager must have entered it wrong, that's all."

"Mmhm," said the detective. She frowned at the kids. "You three, back in the car. Let's go."

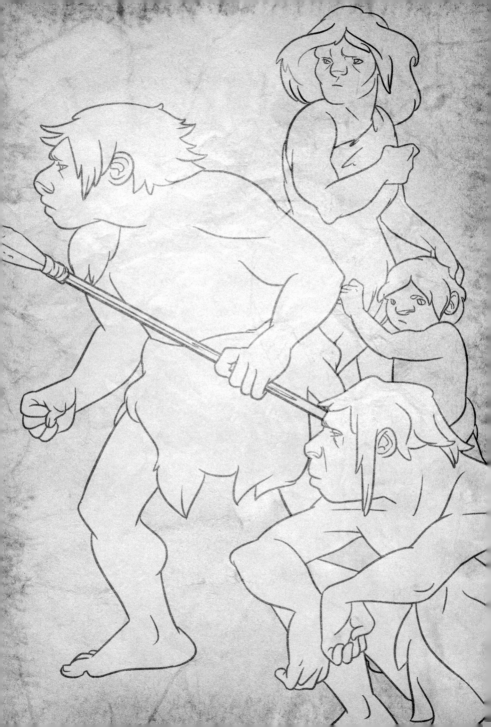

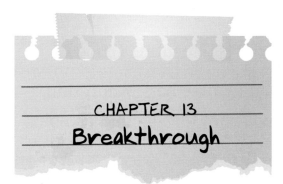

CHAPTER 13
Breakthrough

Detective Pagalucci lectured the kids the whole drive back to the museum. "When I tell you to do something, I *mean* it. I was looking out for your safety," she said. "What if those drivers *had* been the thieves? What if they'd been angry, or dangerous, or *armed*?"

"Sorry, Detective Pagalucci," said Amal, Raining, and Wilson together.

"Sorry," Clementine echoed.

"Don't blame her," Amal said, leaning forward. "She told us not to go."

The detective scowled. "And another thing," she said. "This is a police investigation. I understand you're all very worried about Dr. Kipper, but please let us do our job. No more motel snooping or calling shipping companies, got it?"

"How did you know we called the ship—" Amal started to say, but quickly stopped talking when the detective glared at her. "Sorry."

Detective Pagalucci pulled up to the museum and parked right at the curb.

"Out you go," she said. "I don't want to see you four again today. When I have news for you, I'll track you down. Got it?"

"Got it," Clementine said.

"And you three?" the detective said toward the back seat.

"Got it!" Amal, Raining, and Wilson chimed.

"Good. Now get out of my car," the detective said.

The kids obeyed and hurried into the museum. They spent the rest of the afternoon wandering the halls and galleries, avoiding the investigation at the back of the museum. Eventually, Wilson fell behind. When Clementine noticed, she stopped and waited for him.

"You okay?" she asked.

Wilson wasn't. He sat on the nearest bench, in front of the sunset mural, and shook his head. Clementine sat beside him.

"I really like Detective Pagalucci," she said. "She's a little intense, but I think that's good in a detective. I think she's going to solve this case."

Wilson didn't answer. He just stared straight ahead at that mural.

"There are a bunch of clues now too," Clementine went on. "There's the shipping company truck. There's the blue paint. We should probably interrogate Matthew in maintenance too. He seems so *nice*, though."

"The blue paint," Wilson said suddenly. He jumped to his feet. "This mural you hate. It has blue in it."

"What?" Clementine said, sounding confused. "Ugh, yes. What a terrible blue. It's way too dark. And it clashes with the green of that tree. Don't even get me started on that tree! It's horrendous. It looks like someone who's never painted before — what are you doing?"

Wilson walked toward the exhibit and stepped over the velvet rope. He carefully passed the crouching cavemen discovering fire and walked right up to the mural. Then he ran his palm over the painting. "It's still wet," he said.

"Really?" Clementine said. She stood up too and walked toward the mural.

"Wilson, you're not supposed to be back there."

Wilson knocked on the mural like it was a door. "Hello?" he said.

A security guard on her rounds stepped into the Prehistoric Humans exhibit. "Wilson Kipper?" she said. "You know to stay behind the velvet ropes! Come out of there at once!"

But Wilson ignored her. Instead he pounded his fist on the mural. "Mom?" he shouted. "Mom, are you in there?"

That's when it clicked for Clementine. Her eyes darted around the room and fell upon the posts holding the velvet rope. She grabbed the nearest one and raised it like a baseball bat.

"What are you doing?" the guard shouted, running toward her. "Miss, you put that down right now!"

Clementine ignored her. She barreled toward the mural, let loose a great scream like a Viking warrior, and smashed the base of the post against the mural. Nothing happened.

"Stop!" the guard shouted, but she got tripped up in the fallen velvet rope.

Clementine struck the wall again. This time, it splintered.

"Mom!" Wilson shouted again. "We're coming to get you!"

Clementine smashed — again and again and again — until the wall fell apart in splinters and foam and chunks of wood. As she smashed and smashed, a crowd of curious museumgoers gathered behind her, including Amal and Raining.

"We're here!" came the voice of Dr. Carolyn Kipper. Her face suddenly appeared in the opening Clementine had created. "We're here! You've found us!"

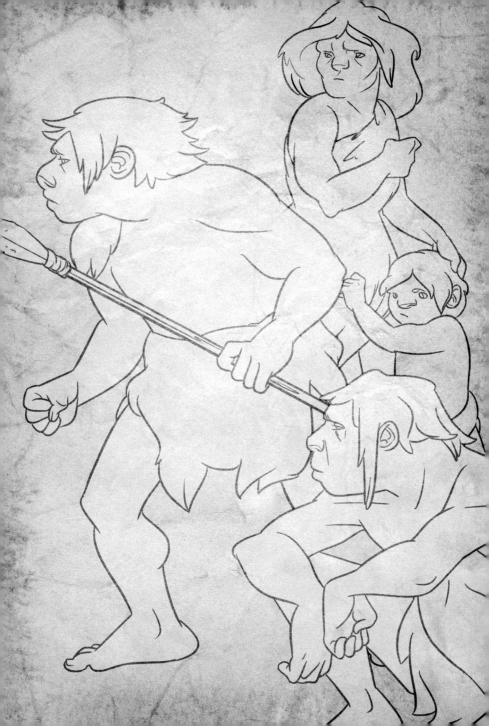

CHAPTER 14
Future Detectives

In no time at all, Matthew from building maintenance took apart the rest of the false wall, revealing the little room behind it where all five of the missing scientists had been tied up. They were hungry, hot, tired, and scared.

"We tried screaming and banging," Dr. Kipper said. She sat on the floor in the

Prehistoric Humans exhibit with her son on her lap and Moman beside them. "But it was no use. They'd packed the walls with soundproofing and foam a foot thick. No one could hear us."

"How did you figure it out, Wilson?" Detective Pagalucci said.

"Mostly thanks to my friends," Wilson said. "Especially Clementine."

Clementine's eyes went wide and her face went red. "Me? What did I do?"

"Well, you smashed the wall, for one thing," Wilson said. "But before that, you knew the mural was the work of an amateur, not of a museum employee."

"True," Clementine said. "But I didn't know why."

"The question now is," the detective said, "who did this to you? We have Matthew from maintenance in custody for questioning right now."

"Matthew?" Dr. Kipper said. "Of course it wasn't Matthew!"

"But the blue paint used in the mural is from his equipment room," the detective said. "Who else could it have been?"

Before Dr. Kipper could answer, Amal said casually, "Isn't it obvious? The delivery guys out at the motel."

"But we already checked their room," Detective Pagalucci said. "And you three checked the truck. If they have the shipment, I don't see where they could have stashed it."

"Fake wall," Amal said, knocking her knuckles on the remaining fragments of wood. "Fake bed."

"Fake bed?" the detective said, sounding confused. Then she snapped her fingers. "Fake bed! Of course!"

"I don't get it," Clementine said. "What fake bed?"

"You were still in the car," Amal said, "but the motel room the drivers were in had an extra bed."

"An extra bed," Clementine repeated, her eyes lighting up as she caught on, "that was really the shipment!"

"With blankets and sheets and pillows on it," the detective said. "It's actually kind of brilliant." She turned to two of her officers standing nearby. "Let's go get 'em."

"What about us?" Wilson asked, sitting up in his mom's lap. "We're the ones who solved it!"

The detective sighed. "Against my better judgment," she said, "fine. You can come. But this time, you stay in the car — *all* of you!"

The kids exchanged excited grins and followed Detective Pagalucci out to her vehicle. When they arrived back at the motel, they did stay in the car this time — all crunched together in the backseat with the doors locked.

They watched as the officers arrested both drivers, who'd been in the process of loading the crates from China back into the shipping truck. Amal opened the window to listen.

"Please, detective," one of the drivers said. "We didn't want to hurt anyone."

"That's why we went back late at night," the second driver added. "We thought the place would be deserted. How were we supposed to know all those scientists would be working late?"

"They knew our faces!" said the first. "We couldn't just let them go report us."

"So you locked them in a padded wooden box," the detective said as she snapped the handcuffs on the crooks.

"Better than hurting them, isn't it?" the first driver said.

"It's still kidnapping," the detective said. "Five counts. Not to mention grand larceny. That shipment was worth millions."

"Don't we know it!" said the other driver. "Our buyer was going to pay us really well! Um, we're going away for a long time, aren't we?"

"A long, *long* time," Detective Pagalucci confirmed. She led them to the other police car, pushed them inside, and thumped the roof. The car drove off, undoubtedly heading for jail.

With the crooks safely disposed of, Detective Pagalucci climbed back into her own unmarked car. "You kids sure impressed me today," she said. "You ever think about becoming detectives when you grow up? We could use some strong minds on the force."

"I don't know," Raining said. "This mystery-solving business is pretty exhausting."

"Besides," Wilson said, thinking about Mom and Moman, "I'm only ten. I don't plan to grow up for a very long time."

Steve B.

About the Author

Steve Brezenoff is the author of more than fifty middle-grade chapter books, including the Field Trip Mysteries series, the Ravens Pass series of thrillers, and the Return to Titanic series. In his spare time, he enjoys video games, cycling, and cooking. Steve lives in Minneapolis with his wife, Beth, and their son and daughter.

Lisa W.

About the Illustrator

Lisa K. Weber is an illustrator currently living in Oakland, California. She graduated from Parsons School of Design in 2000 and then began freelancing. Since then, she has completed many print, animation, and design projects, including graphic novelizations of classic literature, character and background designs for children's cartoons, and textiles for dog clothing.

GLOSSARY

ancient (AYN-shuhnt) — very old or belonging to a time long ago

evidence (EV-uh-duhnss) — information and facts that help prove something or make you believe that something is true

exhibit (eg-ZIB-it) — a public display of works of art, historical objects, etc.

forensic (FUH-ren-sik) — using science to help investigate or solve crimes; a forensic investigation uses fingerprints, blood tests, handwriting analysis, etc.

fossil (FOSS-uhl) — the remains or traces of an animal or a plant from millions of years ago, preserved as rock

fragile (FRAJ-il) — delicate or easily broken

mural (MYU-ruhl) — a painting on a wall

paleontology (pale-ee-uhn-TOL-uh-jee) — the science that deals with fossils and other ancient life-forms; someone who studies paleontology is called a paleontologist.

prehistoric (pree-hi-STOR-ik) — belonging to a time before history was recorded in written form

suspect (SUHSS-peckt) — someone thought to be responsible for a crime

DISCUSSION QUESTIONS

1. Do you think Wilson, Clementine, Amal, and Raining were right to interfere in the investigation, even after the detective told them not to? Talk about why or why not.

2. Who else did you consider as a suspect while reading this story? Talk about your ideas and other suspects' possible motives.

3. Detective Pagalucci suggests the friends consider careers as detectives. Do you think this would be an interesting career? Talk about your opinion.

WRITING PROMPTS

1. Clementine is a great friend to Wilson when he's upset about his mom. Write a paragraph about a time a friend comforted you or vice versa.

2. Wilson, Clementine, Amal, and Raining all have parents who work at museums in Capitol City. Imagine your parent works at a museum. What type of a museum would you find most interesting? Write a paragraph explaining your choice.

3. Imagine you are Wilson's mother or one of the other paleontologists who were trapped by the crooks. Write a paragraph about your experience and how you felt while trapped.

MORE ABOUT PALEONTOLOGY

Paleontology is a science full of mystery — mainly because for as much as fossils tell us about our past, they can't tell us everything. Even so, paleontologists attempt to learn about living things such as plants and animals that existed billions of years ago using fossils.

Fossils are the remains or traces of animals or plants from millions of years ago, preserved as rock, and can include everything from bones, teeth, and shells to footprints. When pieced together, these things paint a picture of how the planet and different species have evolved over time and how they are related to one another. Paleontologists studying fossils are looking to determine three main things: the identity and origin of the fossil, the fossil's environment, and what a particular fossil can tell us about the history of the earth.

Early Fossil Discoveries:

1676 — A huge thigh bone is discovered in England by Reverend Plot. At the time, this was assumed to be from a "giant" but was likely from a dinosaur.

1787 — The first dinosaur fossil in the United States, a thigh bone, is discovered by Dr. Caspar Wistar in Gloucester County, New Jersey.

1838 — The first nearly complete dinosaur skeleton is discovered on the John E. Hopkins Farm in Haddonfield, New Jersey, by William Parker Foulke.

1854 — The first dinosaur models, life-size and made of concrete, are created by Benjamin Waterhouse Hawkins in England.

While paleontologists have found thousands of fossils across the world, the reality is, most fossils may never be found. Some fossils may be buried too deep, while others have probably been destroyed over time by heat and pressure from the earth itself. Still, plenty of fossils have been found, and new ones are being discovered all the time. Each year, paleontologists continue to use these discoveries to piece together the stories of the past.